T0082381

DATELINE MEMPHIS

A NICHELLE CLARKE CRIME THRILLER NOVELLA

LYNDEE WALKER

SEVERN RIVER PUBLISHING

Severn River Publishing
www.SevernRiverBooks.com

This is a work of fiction. Names, characters, businesses, places, events and incidents are either the products of the author's imagination or used in a fictitious manner. Any resemblance to actual persons, living or dead, or actual events is purely coincidental.

ISBN: 978-1-64875-521-7 (Paperback)

ALSO BY LYNDEE WALKER

The Nichelle Clarke Series

Front Page Fatality

Buried Leads

Small Town Spin

Devil in the Deadline

Cover Shot

Lethal Lifestyles

Deadly Politics

Hidden Victims

Dangerous Intent

The Faith McClellan Series

Fear No Truth

Leave No Stone

No Sin Unpunished

Nowhere to Hide

No Love Lost

Tell No Lies

To find out more about LynDee Walker and her books, visit

severnriverbooks.com/authors/lyndee-walker

EDITOR'S NOTE

While the mysteries in the Nichelle Clarke series can be read in any order, readers who like to follow the overall story time-line strictly should read DATELINE MEMPHIS as Nichelle #2.5, between BURIED LEADS and SMALL TOWN SPIN.

A version of this story was previously published as part of the novella anthology *Heartache Motel,* which is no longer in print.

1

Christmas vacation lesson number one: don't leave hotel reservations to chance, especially when visiting a major tourist attraction. Lesson two: crime reporters don't get holidays. Criminals, it turns out, are everywhere.

I committed the first of those to memory before I technically stepped foot in Memphis, sitting in my little SUV fifteen miles west of Graceland behind a run-down Denny's wannabe.

"This is the only place in town with an available room?" I asked my toy Pomeranian, who was strapped into her carrier in the backseat. The boarded-up window punctuating the stucco facade of the Heartache Motel gave it a menacing air in the fading daylight. I wondered about the odds of catching something horrifying from the "deluxe bathroom with shower" advertised on the sign.

Maybe it was just the only available room with an Elvis theme, since that was the only requirement I'd given the operator. Arriving to find the official Elvis hotel had been booked since August left me scrambling.

Whatever. It was only one night. I inherited my mom's love

of classic rock, and was more excited than a kid headed for Disneyland to be stopping at Graceland on my way home to Dallas for Christmas.

Plus, it wasn't the scariest building I'd ever set foot in. In more than half a decade covering crime, I'd ventured into some seedy digs.

"And they do take pets." I turned and smiled at Darcy, who looked happy to have the car parked.

With the dog tucked under one arm and my overnight bag slung over the other, I walked through the glass doors, which were outlined with washed-out Christmas lights. An ancient, peeling Triple-A diamond sticker was the only evidence of better days.

The lobby stank of cigarette smoke and something else I didn't try too hard to place, the sixties-style furniture matching the C-9 bulbs in worn-out sadness. A positively pitiful tree leaned in the far corner, one half-functional strand of orange lights draped around it. Droopy garlands dangled from the walls with the "throw it up and see what sticks" look of al-dente pasta.

I smothered a guffaw when my eyes landed on a gilt-framed velvet Elvis on the wall near the front desk. "They're not serious," I whispered to Darcy. She sniffed the air and tucked her face under one paw.

I was just about to spin back for the door—the Elvis theme wasn't that important—when a deep voice with an obviously-affected feminine lilt stopped me in my tracks. "Can I help you?"

I turned to find the biggest, bustiest, most spectacular drag queen I'd ever laid eyes on. Not that I saw drag queens every day, but I had done a story on a bar frequented by them in college. Some of the nicest folks I'd ever met.

The queen behind the registration desk was a full head

taller than me—and in my stilettos, I touch six-three—with red-orange hair teased into a bouffant that probably required enough White Rain to eat a hole in the ozone right over top of this joint. She had a dainty brown mole on the bow of her top lip, a thick layer of blue eyeshadow, at least three sets of false eyelashes, and cracked true-red lipstick outlining an earnest smile. Her square-necked orange top matched the era of the lights and furniture.

She gave the dingy little Heartache Motel a certain level of awesome. How many hotels have a seven-foot drag queen with a sweet-tea smile working the front desk?

"I called about a half-hour ago," I said, smiling and striding to the desk. "I got your last room, I think? Nichelle Clarke."

"Welcome to Memphis, darlin'," she drawled, pushing a paper across the desk. "I'm Man-Margaret, and you're in our Love Me Tender suite."

"And you said pets are okay?" I asked, looping Darcy's leash around my wrist and setting her down so I could fill out a registration card that looked older than my mom. I jotted my cell number in the top corner and printed my address in Richmond on the faded red lines.

"Dogs and cats, sure. Some asshole brought a snake in here last summer and the damned thing got out and hasn't ever been seen again, so no exotic animals. I ask you, who the hell keeps a python as a pet? Weirdos."

"Different strokes and all that, I guess," I said, grinning. "Which floor?"

"The fifth. The top floor is always the best, like Elvis said." She winked. "Drink specials and menus are in the TV stand. There's a nightly show in the bar. Enjoy, and merry Christmas."

I grabbed the key—a real one on a pink, heart-shaped fob

with what probably used to be the hotel's address in faded gold print—and turned for the elevator.

"It's too bad we don't have a travel section anymore," I muttered as the doors rattled open. "This place would make a hell of a feature story."

As if on cue, my cell phone binged a text from my editor. "Having fun yet? Crime doesn't take holidays, you know."

I shook my head. Bob had been giving me shit for taking this week off since before Thanksgiving. It was good-natured. Mostly.

"R&R is good for productivity, chief. Try it sometime," I tapped.

The elevator opened and I scrunched my nose at the stale-B.O. smell. "Gross. Haven't these folks heard of Febreeze?"

The lights flickered when the doors closed. I studied the green walls as we lurched upward—until I figured out I was squinting at a crude drawing of some kind of advanced tantric-sex move. Everywhere I pointed my eyes I found another, with a few misspelled dirty words sprinkled in for good measure. Before I'd deciphered them all, the elevator wheezed and the doors rattled open to a hallway that belonged in a Stephen King movie.

"Stairs. Definitely the stairs." I would've kissed the red shag carpet in the hall if it hadn't smelled not-so-faintly of urine and smoke.

Darcy growled at a flickering light as I picked my way to room five-twenty-eight. I shoved the key into the lock and jiggled it, then turned the tarnished brass handle and pushed the door open.

The fluorescent overhead fixture only turned halfway on, but it was enough to decide I probably didn't want to see the Love Me Tender suite in any better light.

The whole room was decorated in a bad cowboy theme,

down to the cacti mural on the walls and the faux (I hoped) barbed wire outlining the mirrors. The back of the door was home to a cracked stick-on of young Elvis on horseback. Life-sized. Watching me sleep. Yay.

I put Darcy down, folding her carrier top back and making her a little bed. She looked around, sniffed the carpet and the leg of the lone chair, and shot me a *you-cannot-be-serious* look before she hopped into her bed and curled up.

I tossed my bag onto the round bed. The saddle-printed spread slid to one side and revealed sheets I was sure weren't actual satin in an unfortunate vomit-brown hue. Lovely.

"This place is sold out? Really? Who knew Memphis was a Christmas tourist destination?" I said to stick-on Elvis and my dog. The clerk at Graceland's hotel had apologetically explained that holiday pilgrimages were a fan tradition because Elvis loved Christmastime. My cell-phone operator search for an Elvis theme and a reasonable rate had led here. That operator might get a call back in the morning.

I filled Darcy's water bowl and spooned some Pro Plan into her food dish. She eyed the carpet like she didn't want to step on it again, but gave in because she was hungry.

My phone buzzed another text. Bob again: *I can rest when I'm dead. I have Shelby covering a turkey fryer fire while my cops reporter is gallivanting around Tennessee.*

I rolled my eyes. *Always on the lookout for a headline, chief. This place I'm staying ... I may find one*, I tapped back.

Watching Darcy wolf her food down made my stomach rumble. It had been a long time since my chicken salad lunch, but the thought of getting back in my car was less appealing than sleeping with an empty stomach. Man-Margaret had mentioned a bar. Maybe it had food.

I put a puppy mat on the floor next to Darcy and went to find out.

Suspicious Minds looked as seedy as it sounded, and I wondered idly how much interesting reading I'd find in the FBI database with a fingerprint kit and ten minutes alone in there. Every table was full, the clientele not shy about their drinking from the way the waitresses—all dressed like starlets from Elvis movies—were running. The crowd ranged from Elvis wannabes and fans (most of them in t-shirts emblazoned with the King's face) to a table of large men who looked like they'd be equally at home under a hot rod or in a tattoo parlor.

The bartender had her back to me, a black spaghetti-strapped tank dress showing off chiseled shoulders, topped by a perfectly-pouffed chestnut flip.

"Be right with you," she said in a voice way too deep for a woman who wasn't Kathleen Turner.

She turned with a bright smile, and I grinned. "Good evening, Miss Natalie."

She was a muscular photocopy of Natalie Wood from *All The Fine Young Cannibals*. Which wasn't an Elvis movie, but I knew my pop history. The King and the actress had a fling back in the day.

She nodded. "Charmed, sugar. What you hankering for tonight?" She had a lisp that disappeared into another dazzling grin.

"Food. And sleep."

She pushed a menu across the black leather bar. "We do a mean peanut butter and banana sandwich. Pretty good grilled ham and cheese, too."

Elvis's love of peanut butter and bananas was legend, and I was a fan. I scanned the menu. "I'll take a Hunka PB Love and a diet coke, please."

She jotted the order down and pushed it through a window behind her, then poured my soda into a tall glass.

"Where you in from, sugar?" she asked, her accent more deep south than I'd expect in Memphis.

"Richmond. I'm on my way home for Christmas, but I'm stopping by Graceland to grab a gift for my mom on the way through town."

"First time?"

I nodded. "Mom and I are big Elvis fans. I feel like a kid on her way to Disneyland. I bet I don't get five minutes of sleep."

"Enjoy. 'Scuse me a second." She turned to a thin man with a pompadour and a flipped-up collar at the near end of the bar, and I looked around and sipped my Coke, tapping the heel of one chestnut Louboutin bootie—my latest eBay score —on the leg of the barstool.

At the far end of the bar, next to the flashing Elvis pinball machine, a large man in an apron and a hairnet leaned on one elbow, deep in conversation with a busty woman with big blond hair, an Elvis Lives crop top, and a Santa hat. I watched them, never sure if my curiosity was an outgrowth of my job or the other way around. Their discussion dissolved to bickering, then she smiled, resting her double-Ds on the bar, and pushed a wad of cash to him. He pulled a small package from under the bar. She palmed it, dropping her hand out of sight. They exchanged a nod and parted ways, him to the kitchen and her to the tattoo-parlor set at the corner table.

"Dealing drugs in plain sight. Nice," I muttered, my attention turning back to my stomach when Natalie set a plate in front of me. I'd seen worse, chasing stories through some questionable establishments. This place thrummed with the junkie-haven vibe.

I smiled a *thank you*, lifting the sandwich and biting through its perfect honey-gold crust. It was seriously the best thing I'd ever eaten. Or I was really hungry. Either way, I snarfed it up in less than three minutes, drained my Coke, and threw a handful of bills on the bar.

Back upstairs, I heard Darcy yapping from halfway down the hall. Sprinting to the door, I flipped the light on, shushing her. She almost never barked.

"Darcy! What's gotten into you?" I hissed, much more politely than the gruff chorus of "shut up, mutt!" echoing in the hallway. She snarled and pawed at the air vent next to her bed.

"Rattly furnace," I sighed, snatching her up and scratching her ears, then moving her bed. She disliked the one in my 1924 craftsman back in Richmond, too.

By the time I took her outside and scrubbed my face in the closet that passed for a "deluxe bathroom," even the vomit-colored sheets looked inviting. I did get more than five minutes of sleep, and I ended up needing every second.

2

I bounced in my seat as the bus turned through the famous musical gates that led to Elvis's mansion, staring at the front of the house as it came into view.

"It's so close to the street," I said to no one in particular, and the lady in the seat in front of me laughed.

"I said that the first time I came here, too," she said in a thick Brooklyn accent. "I love seeing young people who appreciate good music."

I grinned. "I'm a big fan."

The bus stopped and I popped to my feet, hoping Darcy was content to stay quiet with her food and potty pad in the motel room. Not that dog pee was the worst thing to ever happen to that carpet, but still.

"I'm Teresa," the woman said when she stood, turning to show off a Comeback '68 shirt she'd probably purchased during the original tour. She stuck a hand out for me to shake. "Where are you from?"

"Richmond," I said, wondering when that had become my default answer, instead of Dallas. "How about you? New York?"

She nodded. "I moved to Miami about ten years ago. The older I get, the more I despise the cold."

"I'm not fond of it either, but I like coats and boots better than blistering heat and bugs the size of birds," I said. "I grew up in Texas. Not too different from Florida."

She shrugged. "I'm a Brooklyn broad. If New York rats don't scare me, I can handle palmetto bugs."

"I guess so," I said, fiddling with the headset they'd given me at the ticket office. "I'm going to Texas, actually. I stopped to see the sights and grab a souvenir for my mom."

"Well, they have plenty to choose from. I've been here every Christmas since my Murray died in 1998, and they get more stuff every year." She patted a shoulder bag emblazoned with an Andy Warhol-style picture of Elvis. "I'm choosy, after all this time. I have my own towel the King wiped his face on at Madison Square Garden in 1969. Never been washed."

Um, gross.

"This year, I'm collecting coins," she said over her shoulder as we filed off the bus. "Got three on my Elvis wall so far. Good investment and souvenir in one."

"Thanks. I'll keep that in mind." I smiled and turned on my headset, following the crowd up the steps to the front of the house. It was gorgeous, and impeccably maintained, with the Christmas decorations making it grander. I had to admit, though, a few episodes of *Celebrity Cribs* had left me expecting Elvis' home to be much bigger. Not that it was anything to sneeze at, but Dennis Rodman had twice as much square footage, and he was no king of rock 'n roll.

I walked through the front doors, following the honey-voiced narrator in my headset, who took turns with Priscilla Presley describing rooms and telling stories. Marveling at the timeless snowy decor in the living room, I pictured Elvis sitting by the tree strumming a guitar. Just looking at the piano was enough to make me hold my breath for a moment of silence. It was a borderline religious experience, standing in the space that had witnessed the creation of such amazing music. An older couple in front of me in the foyer cracked me up, her bouncing and swatting at his arm over every little thing, and him feigning interest. Poorly, though she either didn't notice or didn't care.

The kitchen was flashback fabulous, with amber glass in the cabinets, Tiffany hanging lamps, and crazy-patterned flooring—and also surprisingly cozy, unlike some of the industrial-looking kitchens I saw in high-dollar homes on TV. I could see myself perching on the barstool and sipping coffee.

People moved through the rooms at different speeds. I noticed uniformed guards in the corners, trying to blend in with the decor. It was probably funny to see all the silent tourists, listening closely to their headphones, wandering around the house.

Cringing, I watched a pair of small boys dart around the china-set dining table. Their mother waved half-hearted objections toward them, which they ignored. I snapped a photo and scooted out before the boys could break anything.

I followed a short set of steps down to the famous Jungle Room, tucked off the kitchen, and stared at the carpeted walls and ceiling and the rock waterfall, feeling the joy hanging heavy in the air deep in my bones as the headset droned about Elvis' affinity for the space.

The second floor of the house, where all the bedrooms except the one that belonged to Elvis' parents are located, is off limits. My headphones directed me downstairs. I clicked the tour off while I walked.

I ducked under a low door facing at the bottom of the staircase and stepped into the basement, nearly walking into a tall man in baggy coveralls carrying a large bin out of a side hallway. "I'm sorry," I said, stepping back and waving him ahead of me.

"My fault. 'Scuse me, ma'am," he said in a heavily southern lisp, smiling and dropping his dark eyes to the floor as he backed up. "Ladies first. Where you headed?"

I stared for a second, his voice ringing familiar for a reason I couldn't place. Talking to so many people each day gave me a good ear for nuance. Then again, with the headphones off it was hard to hear myself think over the people gabbing about various artifacts.

"Just to the rec room, I think." I smiled, scooting around him.

"Enjoy," he said. I spun back, watching as his dark head disappeared up the stairs. Weird.

I turned my headphones back on as I walked into the game room, the headset track telling a story about the nick in the pool table, the product of a wayward bullet fired by a member of Elvis' "Memphis Mafia" group of friends.

The TV room was high-tech for the sixties, with three sets enclosed in a cabinet and a huge lightning-bolt "TCB" logo mural on the wall behind the sectional sofa.

I was almost back to the stairs, ready to go out to the old racquetball court that serves as the trophy room to see Elvis' platinum records, costumes, and awards, when I heard a woman shouting. I clicked pause on the audio tour.

"I don't know which one of you is doing it, but if it doesn't stop today, I'll fire every last one of you," a voice bellowed from behind a heavy door on my left. I resisted the urge to open it, but stayed put, feigning interest in the framed photo of Elvis and his mother on the wall. If what didn't stop? My gut lurched the way it does when I start a big story, and I tried to calm it with a deep breath. For all I knew, Bellow

McYellerson on the other side of the door was pissed about someone eating her ham on rye.

Murmurs of agreement.

"Good. Get back to work," she snapped.

See? I shook my head and reminded myself that I was on vacation. Which meant I wasn't supposed to be looking for a story under every gold record.

Upstairs, I stepped out into the sun, only a little chilly in the warm December weather, detouring to the meditation garden to pay my respects. It was a peaceful resting place, protected, befitting a man who spent half his life trying to hide from his sometimes-rabid fanbase.

From the garden, I passed the small shooting range and stepped into the trophy hall—one wall housed enough gold and platinum to keep a small European country afloat for years. I clicked the recording back on and browsed, surrounded by ogling tourists and beautiful things. I made it back outside, my destination the cars and planes on the other side of Elvis Presley Boulevard, before everything went bonkers.

3

Security guards shouting into walkie-talkies poured from every corner of the property, all running toward the trophy room behind the main house.

I clicked my headphones off and spun on my heel, sprinting after them.

Sure, the ruckus could be because one of the rowdy kids puked on one of Elvis's Grammys. But I didn't think so.

I stopped in front of the costume wall in the awards hall and pulled a notebook and pen from my bag. The guards were clustered around a showcase, and from my spot in the back of the crowd I couldn't see what was in it, but they were freaked about something. The hairs on my arm pricked at the thought that I might be the only reporter on the scene of a breaking story. Merry Christmas to me. Graceland was a national landmark, Elvis a billion-dollar enterprise. Egg nog and cookies could wait.

I wriggled to the front of the small crowd gathered around the guards. Between the tight knot they formed and everyone around me talking at once, I had no way to gauge what was going on. I elbowed my way around the outside of their circle and stood as tall as I could, catching a glimpse of an empty display case. About two-by-three, top lit, and between two of Elvis' most famous stage outfits.

Holy Manolos. If what belonged in there was missing, that was news. I racked my brain, trying to remember what I'd seen in that case not twenty minutes before, but came up with nothing. Except that I'd have noticed if any of the cases were empty. They were not. But how could something that big go missing in the middle of the day?

I took a step back when a tall man in a guard uniform and a big hat stepped forward, holding up his hands for quiet. His teeth flashed white against his olive skin when he offered a reassuring smile. "Ladies and gentlemen, we do apologize for the inconvenience, but I'm afraid the exits to the grounds have been locked for the time being and the Memphis Police will be here shortly. We have a situation. You're all free to continue to move about the grounds, but we ask that if you see anything suspicious, you alert a member of the security team immediately. Y'all enjoy your day." He nodded a dismissal and most of the guards disbanded, leaving a group of curious tourists whispering musings in their wake.

I scribbled notes and fumbled for my cell phone to text my editor in Richmond.

Something up @ Graceland. Security in an uproar. Looks like something's missing from the trophy hall. They locked it down. And I'm in here. I hit send with a shaking finger. God, I hoped he was at the office.

My phone buzzed a reply less than a minute later: *!!!!!!*

I found a bench in a corner where I could still see the guards and the empty case, opening an email to Bob.

· · ·

Security guards at Elvis Presley's Graceland mansion put the complex on lockdown just after noon Friday.

"The Memphis Police will be here shortly," a guard told a small crowd gathered around an empty display case in the trophy hall behind the mansion. "We have a situation."

No further details were given, but tourists were told that they're free to roam the grounds until the police arrive. A Telegraph *reporter is among those locked inside.*

I sent the email and clicked back to my texts. *You have email. I'm on it. I'll send updates as I have them.* Send.

I tucked the phone into the back pocket of my jeans and made my way through the crowd, looking for anyone who might know what was happening.

My backside buzzed a text arrival just as my eyes lit on a petite redhead whose little girl shared her wild curls. The mom was talking to a guard and gesturing between the child and the guards who formed a body wall around the empty case. The guard took notes as he nodded.

It's on the web, Bob's text read. *Keep it coming. I'm camped here.*

Working on it. Send.

I slipped close enough to the guard conducting the interview to eavesdrop.

"She didn't do anything to it," the woman said, her voice escalating in pitch. "She smacked the glass and squealed for me to look. She likes sparkly things."

Smacked the glass? No way all this hysteria was over a cracked cabinet. My eyes strayed back to the human barrier around the case, but the effort was futile. I was too far away and they were too tightly meshed at the shoulders for me to see a thing.

"Ma'am, no one is accusing your little girl of anything," the smooth drawl came from the guard in the hat as he walked up next to me. I swiveled my eyes to the gold records on the far wall and feigned disinterest, but I'm not sure he even noticed me, he was so focused on the pixieish face behind the tangle of auburn ringlets.

Kneeling, the officer asked the child her name.

"Savannah," she chirped.

"I'm Dale. Nice to meet you, Miss Savannah." He held up one hand. "Can I have a high five?"

She reached a tiny arm up and walloped his palm. He flapped his wrist and dropped his jaw in mock-astonishment. "You're a mighty strong little lady," he said, ruffling her hair. "How old are you?"

"Five." She giggled, holding up as many fingers and shaking her head when he insisted she had to be at least seven.

"Can you tell me how many times you hit the glass?"

"Three? Four?" Savannah hung her head. "I wanted mommy to look."

"And what happened when you hit the glass?"

"A sparkle fell," she said, her face scrunching as she tightened her arm around her mother's thigh. "I didn't mean to break it."

"You didn't break anything, sugar. Don't you worry." The first guard scribbled more while the one with the hat—I guessed he was in charge—straightened and nodded at the mother. "If you wouldn't mind giving Calvin here your contact information, ma'am, we'd sure appreciate it. But please don't worry about anything. Y'all have happened into the middle of something much bigger than a—" He touched Savannah's arm and winked, "—'falling sparkle.' You watch that right hook, killer."

He turned back toward the empty case and I followed a few paces behind, still admiring his technique with the kid. What were the odds he'd talk to me? Without a connection, probably not good.

He had a short conference with the guards that I didn't dare creep close enough to overhear, then glanced at his iPhone and walked back outside toward the main house.

I turned back to Savannah and her mother, who were standing alone about halfway down the hallway, looking at a jumpsuit.

I fished my pad and pen back out as I wandered toward them. The woman glanced at me and I smiled.

"Interesting day," I said.

She shook her head. "Not at all what I had in mind when my momma said she wanted to come to Graceland." She gestured to an older woman who was snapping photos of every gold record on the opposite wall.

I offered a hand. "I'm Nichelle," I said. "I'm a reporter. Who's supposed to be on vacation, so I can relate. What was all that about, if you don't mind me asking?" I waved toward the guards.

She shook my hand. "Bonnie. Bonnie McCracken. It was the craziest thing. Savannah banged the glass on that display case to get me to look down, and alarms started going off and security came out of the woodwork and hustled everyone back and took the belt out of there."

"Belt?" I jotted notes as she talked.

"One of the big gold and jeweled ones he wore onstage," Bonnie said. "One of the jewels fell off when Savannah hit the glass, and the whole place went batshit. Er, crazy."

I grinned. "Yes, ma'am."

"I didn't mean to break it," Savannah said in a small voice, and I knelt down.

"I'm sure you didn't," I said, smiling at her. "More than that, I'm sure you're not in trouble."

"Santa will still come to see me?" she threw a glance at her mom, who patted her shoulder.

"I'm sure he wouldn't miss it, sweetie," I said, straightening up.

My brain sped through the possibilities for a lockdown because of a broken costume piece and came up with exactly bupkis. Which meant there was more to the story.

I thanked Bonnie for her time and patted Savannah's head when she smiled up at me, jotting down their hometown before I tucked my notepad back in my bag.

My cell phone buzzed again.

"I'm working on it, chief," I sighed, clicking it on.

Merry Christmas, beautiful. I smiled. Not Bob. Joey. It was still a little weird to get text messages from my sexy Mafia boss friend. Even weirder to feel electricity shoot from my neck to my toes just seeing his name on my phone screen. I wasn't certain what Joey and I were doing. It wasn't like I could settle down and pick out china with Mr. Mystery. But he sure was a good kisser, and he wasn't asking for a commitment.

Merry Christmas, indeed, I tapped. *I'm locked in at Graceland with a breaking story. I must've been a good girl this year.*

While I was at it, I shot my mom a text to tell her I was running late. I left off the "criminals present" part so she wouldn't worry.

Shoving the phone back into my pocket, I walked out into the sunshine, looking for Dale the security guard, and mentally rehearsing an introduction that might not get me stonewalled—or worse, tossed out.

4

After a trip through the garden and one lap through the main floor of the house, I finally spotted Dale talking to a woman in a housekeeping uniform. She was gesturing wildly, as he nodded, taking notes. I hung back and waited for them to finish, wishing I could hear what she was saying, but not wanting to annoy him just before I asked him for a comment.

When he dismissed her and pushed his little notepad back into his pocket, I stepped into his line of sight and smiled.

"Excuse me," I said, putting out one hand. "I know you're busy, and I know you don't know me, but I'm a reporter, and I'm wondering if I might be able to ask you a couple of questions about what's going on here?"

His smile faded, and he stared at my hand for five beats before he shook it. "A reporter?" He gave me a once-over. "For who? I don't recognize you from the TV. And how did you get in here?"

"I cover cops and courts for the *Richmond Telegraph*," I said, handing him my press credentials. "I'm on vacation, actually, and stopped to see the mansion on my way home for Christmas. Or, I was on vacation. I seem to be unable to get away from the news."

"That's unfortunate timing," he muttered, drumming his fingers on his thigh. "Listen, ma'am, I can appreciate that you're trying to do your job, but I also have to do mine. Elvis Presley is more than an icon. He's an institution. And we have very strict policies about security and media folks here."

I grinned. "Mostly that you don't talk to us, right? No one likes bad PR, and I get that. But so far, whatever this is doesn't sound to me like anything that's going to make the mansion look bad."

He smiled back, though he looked like he didn't really want to. "That's not for me to decide, and my boss is on vacation this week," he said. "I'm going to have to follow policy and say 'no comment.' "

I nodded, clicking out my pen. "Can I get your name and title to go with that 'no comment,' officer?"

"Dale. Dale Leonard. I'm acting head of security this week."

I jotted that down and smiled at him. "I'm Nichelle. Thanks for your time. You were good with the little girl out there, too. Nice, getting the high five to see how hard she might have hit the case."

He arched an eyebrow. "You might not need me to talk to you," he said, turning toward a back hallway that looked like it led to offices. "But thanks. Sweet kid. I'm sorry she got caught in this."

"I don't suppose you have any idea when we might get out of here?" I asked, stepping back.

"Not a good one, no." He tipped his hat and walked away.

I sighed as I watched him go. He wasn't an asshole, which was always a consideration when dealing with cops who didn't know me. But he wasn't going to be any help, either.

As I pondered who might be, Teresa's voice came from my elbow.

"What in the name of *Blue Hawaii* is going on here?" she shook her head at me. "I was down in the Jungle Room and some woman came running in and said we're being kept here. I thought she was crazy, but three other people said the same thing and then the little security guy in the dining room confirmed it. Why on God's Earth would they lock five hundred people in Graceland Christmas week? Is somebody dead? You see anything, Richmond?"

"I did, actually," I said. "The problem is, I don't know what it means. It doesn't make any sense, why they'd freak like this over a jewel coming off a belt. No one's saying anything, really, but that's what I have so far."

"What kind of belt?" she asked.

"It was in a case out in the trophy hall." I waved a hand toward the back doors. "The case is empty now. But the lady who saw what happened said they came and took the belt out."

"And then locked the place down?" Teresa asked.

"Seems extreme, right? I don't have all the pieces to this puzzle yet. I'm trying to find them."

"You a cop or something, honey?"

I laughed. "A reporter. I cover cops, when I'm at home. Turns out, news breaks in the strangest places. But I don't have a lot on this yet. You come here pretty often. You know of anyone I can talk to?"

"Hmmmm. Security?"

"Strikeout." I shook my head.

"Housekeeping?"

Dale had been talking to a woman in a housekeeping uniform. Hmmmm. "You think?"

She nodded. "Oh, honey. The maids know everything. My

sister's been a maid at the Plaza for thirty-five years. She can tell you which celebrities are all-designer and which wear knockoffs, and who sleeps with who, who's on a crazy diet— the trick is getting housekeeping to trust you."

I nodded, her words and the memory of another story tickling the back of my brain.

What if the panic wasn't over a broken belt?

What if the belt in the case broke because it was a knock-off? And if so, where was the real one?

"Teresa, you just gave me a great idea." I patted her arm. "If you'll excuse me, I have some work to do, but I'll talk to you in a little while."

"Good luck, doll. I'll be interested to see what you find out." She wandered back toward the dining room and I went back out into the December sunshine, looking for a place to sit and think. I found a porch off what looked like a basement exit, a little bench along one side. The odor and cigarette butt litter told me it was a smoking porch for the staff. Sitting down, I took out my notes, flipping to a fresh page and writing myself a bullet-pointed list.

Dale had told Bonnie and Savannah they'd wandered into something much bigger than a "falling sparkle."

Dale told me I had "unfortunate timing." Which could mean he was irritated by my presence. Or, coupled with the other comment, it could mean I'd wandered into the middle of a bigger investigation.

Of what, though?

The whole place had gone nuts over a broken costume piece. Which seemed stupid. Why would something getting damaged cause a lockdown?

I underlined that, because I thought I had an answer. It wouldn't. No way an outfit like Graceland panics paying customers and risks lawsuits or God knows what else over something like that. Most of the pieces are better than fifty years old, after all. Things break.

But a stolen one? What if someone took a belt that Elvis actually wore, and replaced it with a replica that fell apart when an excited little girl banged on the glass case? And we were all locked in here because Dale and company believed the real thing was still somewhere on the property?

That was a pretty sexy story. But I needed more than my gut to send it to Bob. How could I get proof when security was freezing me out?

I tapped the heel of one boot on the concrete, so lost in thought I almost jumped out of my skin when the door to my right opened. My bag dumped onto the ground, and I bent to pick up the jumble of papers, loose change, pens, and lip gloss that bounced across the concrete.

"Missed one." The drawl was naggingly familiar. I paused, trying to place it before I met the dark eyes of the man in the coveralls I'd almost run over that morning in the hallway. Still nothing.

"Thanks." I smiled, stuffing a pink lip gloss tube back into my bag.

"You wander off the tour?"

"Just looking for a quiet place to think," I said.

"Some kind of mess goin' on here today." He leaned against the wall and folded his arms over his chest.

"There is that," I said. "I was kind of trying to figure it out."

"You a cop or somethin'?" He tilted his head to one side.

I laughed. "Not in these shoes. I'm a reporter."

"You don't say? Where you from?"

"Richmond. What about you?"

"Born and raised in Tupelo." He flashed a dazzling grin, his angular face lighting up.

I eyed his gray-green coveralls. "What do you do here?"

"Groundskeeping. Not as much work in the winter as in the warmer months, so we run a smaller crew. I was s'posed to get out of here at noon. Goin' home for Christmas a few days early. Now I'm stuck for Lord knows how long."

"Have you heard anything about what's going on?"

He stared at me for a long minute. "Not really. Somethin' missin', I think. People are whisperin'. Security haulin' people in for questionin'." He stuffed his hands in his pockets, the coveralls pulling around his midsection.

"I see." I stood up, smiling again. "I hope you get home soon. Merry Christmas."

"Merry Christmas."

I walked laps around the fence outlining the meditation garden. "Something missing," he'd said. But an offhand comment from a gardener wasn't confirmation enough to print anything. At home, I'd find a way to wheedle it out of someone at the PD. But I didn't know anyone at the Memphis PD.

Did I know anyone who might?

"Damn, Nichelle," I muttered, fishing out my cell phone. "Slow today, aren't we?"

I opened my contacts and found Kyle Miller's cell phone number. My long-ago ex was a federal agent with the Bureau of Alcohol, Tobacco, Firearms, and Explosives. He was already at his parents' house in Dallas, which I knew because they'd invited me over for caroling the following night. But he had law enforcement contacts all over the country, and the Christmas spirit might put him in the mood to share one with me.

"Ho, ho, ho," he said when he picked up. "You on your way yet? How's Elvis?"

"I am not," I said. "I'm working on a story and I need a

favor." Beating around the bush with Kyle usually didn't get me anywhere.

"Working? Come on, Nicey! It's Christmas! I thought you were coming over tomorrow night. My mom is making white chocolate cookies and fondue, and she's so excited to see you she hasn't talked about much else since I got here. You know my folks love you."

I smiled. "I love them, too. I intend to get there, but I have to finish this. I've found crime doesn't respect the calendar, Mr. Federal Agent."

"It does wait, though."

"Not today. I'm locked in at Graceland. I'm pretty sure something's been stolen from the trophy hall. There's an empty showcase that used to house one of Elvis's stage belts. Now, the people who saw what happened said a jewel fell off it and security whisked it away, but my money's on the fact that the jewel coming loose tipped someone to the fact that it was fake, and they locked the gates to try to keep the real one here until they can find the thief. Mostly because it's the only scenario that makes sense, given the things I've seen and heard. Of course, I can't get confirmation of that. Security's not talking and the Memphis PD isn't here yet. That I've seen, anyway. I'm hoping you know someone who can help me out."

"Locked in? Like they sealed the grounds?" Kyle couldn't keep the curiosity out of his voice.

"Hard to keep that vacation mindset when there's an interesting case, isn't it?" I teased.

I could practically see his ice-blue eyes roll skyward. "I just don't want to disappoint my mom. We have an office in Memphis. Let me make a couple calls and see if I can come up with anything."

I pumped a fist in the air. "Thanks, Kyle. I owe you."

"Ten years worth of Christmas gifts, right?" He laughed,

and something tingled in the pit of my stomach. I'd once thought Kyle Miller was the love of my life, and he'd walked back into it at the craziest time. I was looking forward to seeing him more than I wanted to admit, even to myself.

I thanked him again and clicked off the call, crossing my fingers and perching on another concrete bench, opening an email to Bob. I wanted to get the story ready to send if I could someone to confirm my theory.

A priceless piece of music history was stolen from Graceland mansion in Memphis Friday, prompting a lockdown of the property while the investigation unfolded.

"Cop quote here,"

I typed the space-saver after the lead and paused. The only reason for the lockdown was if they thought the belt hadn't left the grounds, right?

So either I was right and the one in the case was a fake, or someone had made off with it after they'd pulled it out of the case, while security was scrambling to seal exits and find witnesses.

"Security haulin' people in for questionin'," The gardener, whose name I hadn't asked, had said.

I'd seen Dale talking to a woman in a housekeeping uniform. And I'd heard someone shouting that morning, before everything went nuts. What had that woman said? Something about firing people if something didn't stop.

I checked my watch. It had been 45 minutes, and I felt the clock ticking. I needed an inside source, and Kyle might not be able to find anyone. It was Christmas week, after all. And Bob had put my first story on the web almost an hour before. I might be the only reporter in here, but what if someone had a cousin on the staff or something? I wanted it first. Especially with my beat being babysat by the copy chief who spent her days gunning for my job— and her nights sleeping with anyone she thought could help her get it.

I saved the email draft and tucked the phone back into my pocket, wondering where I might find a chatty housekeeper.

5

I wandered back to the smoking porch where I'd talked to the gardener, ducking inside the door he'd come out. Fixing a confused-tourist expression on my face, I looked around. I was in a long, sterile hallway that looked like a work area. I walked slowly in the direction of the main area of the basement, keeping my eyes and ears out for anyone in a maid's uniform.

I made it to the far end of the hall without seeing another soul. I sighed, ready to call strike one, when I heard a clatter on the other side of a closed door. I paused.

"You said this would work out," a shrill voice wailed.

"Shhh! You want someone to hear you?" The second one was almost too quiet to pick up, but I'm pretty practiced at eavesdropping (occupational hazard). I got enough to piece the sentence together.

"I can't spend Christmas in jail!" The first woman was only a little quieter that time.

"Will you calm down? What does anyone know? Nothing. And as long as we don't tell them anything, that's what they'll keep knowing. Just hold it together until we get out of here."

"And then what? You think they'll just give up?"

"I think it was Christmas money and Christmas is pretty much over. They'll give up eventually."

The door handle rattled and I scuttled through the thick door at the end of the hall, striding through the basement to the rec room before I stopped walking.

Holy Manolos.

I hadn't seen them, and they hadn't said their names, but that sounded pretty damning. I looked around, wondering where acting head of security Dale had gotten off to. And if he might know who they were. Maybe policy said he couldn't talk to me on the record, but he might be willing to swap some information if I didn't reveal my source.

A quick search didn't find him lurking in the basement. I took the stairs back to the main floor two at a time, my thoughts racing. I'd just stepped into the hallway when my cell phone started buzzing. I pulled it out and checked the screen. Kyle.

"This just keeps getting more interesting," I said in place of hello.

"Sorry I'm missing all the fun." He chuckled. "I did find you an in at the Memphis PD. Lionel Pierce. He's a detective in their major crimes unit. No idea if this is his case or not, but he might be able to get you someone who will talk to you. Merry Christmas. You saved me a trip to the shoe store."

"This could be better than shoes." I scribbled the detective's name down. "And I don't say that about many things. You didn't happen to get a cell number for me, did you?"

"Of course I did," he said, his voice dropping to a sexy baritone. "What's it worth to you?"

I laughed in spite of myself. "We can discuss that when I get there," I said, memories of long-ago Christmases with Kyle tugging at my heart. But I could worry about my flummoxed love life after I got the story.

"All right. I trust you to keep your word."

Butterflies flapped around in my belly before he reeled off the number.

"Thanks, Kyle. I'll see you soon."

I hung up and shoved thoughts of a fireside heart-to-heart (and fantasies about where that could lead) to the back of my brain as I retreated to a quiet corner to call Detective Pierce. I crossed my fingers as I hit "send," hoping he wasn't on vacation like the rest of the world.

I must've been on Santa's "extra good" list, because he answered on the second ring and was surprisingly jovial for a guy working over the holidays.

"My man Jeff at the ATF office says you're trustworthy," Pierce said in a gravelly tenor. "That's high praise for a reporter. What do you need to know about Memphis?"

"I'm locked in at Graceland," I said. "I need to know what the hell's going on here and why hundreds of people are being held on the grounds. It's only been an hour, but folks are starting to get antsy. It's going to get ugly if this goes on much longer. The guard I talked to said they're waiting for the Memphis PD to show up. So anything you can tell me about any of the above would be fantastic."

I heard keys tapping in the background.

"We don't show a call from Graceland today," he said. "Who told you the grounds were locked?"

Come again?

"The acting head of security," I said. "There's something funky going on with a belt in the trophy hall that started the whole thing. Maybe it's just not in the system yet?" My voice went up at the end of that sentence, turning it into a question as I thought about Dale's smooth demeanor and easy smile. Shit. Did security have access to display cases? What if it was him?

"Our systems update automatically," Pierce said. "But there's one more place I can look. Stand by, please."

All I heard for several minutes was the soft *clickety-clack* of computer keys.

"There," he said finally. "There is an open file on Grace-land, but it's in property. Let me see when they should have a car out there." More clicking. "Oh. No, that's something else."

"There's another case file about Graceland? In the property crimes division?" My story radar went on high alert.

"It appears they're working a switch scam involving limited edition Elvis coins at the gift shop there," Pierce said. "But I can't comment on it further. It's not my case, and this file is password-protected."

"Is that standard procedure?" His tone told me it wasn't, but I needed him to say it.

"No, ma'am."

I scribbled, my brain racing. Stolen coins, passworded files at the PD, and people locked in the mansion when the police computer had no record of a call. What the everloving hell?

"A switch-scam?" I asked.

"I can't comment further," he repeated.

"Detective Pierce, I really appreciate your time and help, and believe me, I understand the spot you're in. You don't know me from Ann Margaret. But this is a very unusual situation, and anything you can tell me, even off the record, would really be helpful." I took a deep breath.

He was quiet for a second. "Off the record?"

"Absolutely."

"I don't like that I can't find a call in the system about the lockdown. And I can't speak to this coin case in particular, but things like that are usually counterfeiting operations. Either someone took the real coins and replaced them with fakes, or they were never there in the first place. I can't even see where the report originated, so I don't know if we got a call from the mansion or from a pissed-off collector."

He paused, typing more. I scribbled.

"Moreover, I can't find a report on stolen ones being fenced," Pierce continued. "Which is weird, because this first one was months ago. When people steal collector's items, they sell them. Usually online."

I noted that.

"That actually fits with the theory I've been able to piece together," I said. "Best I can tell, security figured out that one of the big gold costume belts in the trophy room was a fake. They scooted it out of the case before I got a look at it. I'm guessing they think the real one is still here, though. Why else would they seal the exits?"

He was quiet for a minute.

"Detective?"

"Off the record, I'd say you're probably onto something."

Score one for the crime reporter. "Can I get the correct spelling of your name for my article?" I asked.

He gave it to me. "Just so we're clear, you're not printing anything except that we have an open investigation there, correct?"

"Yes, sir."

"Good. About this lockdown—I'm going to create a file, because we don't seem to have one. You said you've been locked in for an hour?"

"Yes, sir." I gave him my name and cell number for the report.

"We're short-staffed because of the holiday, but this is more pressing than what I was doing when you called. I'll stay with it. If I turn anything up, I'll call you back."

"I really appreciate that," I said. "I have a feeling I'm going to end up owing my friend at the ATF a favor."

"Good, then he can owe me one." Pierce laughed. "Watch your back, Miss Clarke. And call if you see anything we need to know about. I'm betting it'll be at least an hour before I can get someone there for a theft, but I'll put it in."

"I will. Thanks, detective. And Merry Christmas."

I hung up, leaning my head back against the wall and closing my eyes. Well, shit. So much for finding Dale and asking about the mysterious women I'd overheard bickering downstairs. Whatever happened to normal crime stories where the players were who they seemed?

I reopened the email I'd started to Bob and stared at the lead.

I deleted "was stolen" and replaced it with "went missing," because after talking to Pierce, I really wasn't sure what I was dealing with. It seemed on the surface like they wouldn't have locked the grounds unless the belt had been stolen, and unless they were still pretty sure it was there. But then why had Dale announced that the police had been called if they hadn't been? Then again, why on Earth would he lock down the complex if he was the thief?

The best I had for that was that he'd get busted for not following procedure, which might raise suspicion. And sounded totally plausible. But that also meant I wasn't asking him about anything else.

And the women downstairs—what the heck were they talking about if Dale was the culprit? Had I strolled into a crime ring situation?

Oy. I didn't have any answers. I needed to send Bob an update, though, and from what Pierce had said, I was running out of time. Once the police filed a report, my exclusive would disappear faster than last season's Louboutins on Black Friday.

I clicked the phone screen back to life and started typing.

· · ·

"[The property crimes division is] working a switch scam involving limited edition Elvis coins at the gift shop there," Detective Lionel Pierce of the Memphis Police Department said. He had no comment on the lockdown or any other open investigations.

Graceland security was tight-lipped about the situation, too.

"No comment," said Acting Head of Security Dale Leonard, citing a policy forbidding security contact with the media. Leonard said he wasn't sure how long the lockdown would last.

Pierce said Memphis Police would be en route as soon as possible, but since the situation wasn't an emergency, short staffing because of the holidays could mean a long response time.

I contemplated that for a few seconds, but left it that way. On the off chance anyone trapped in here with me saw the story on their smartphone, I didn't want to start a riot by revealing that the cops hadn't been told we were being kept here until I called. Since no other reporter would have reason to know that, I could save it for after everyone was safely on their way home.

I added the gardener's comment about people being hauled in for questioning and cited him as an unnamed source, so I wouldn't get him in hot water with Dale.

I hit send and gave it a second, then called Bob.

"I was just about to get worried," he said.

"I'm starting to do a little of that, myself." I gave him the rundown of my situation, picturing his bushy white eyebrows raising by degrees as I talked.

"Holy *Blue Christmas*, kiddo," he said. "Only you. I've been on lots of vacations. I haven't ever stumbled into a whopper of a headline on one, though. You have a knack."

"I'd rather have a knack for cooking. Or gardening. Or sniffing out deals on shoes."

"No, you wouldn't. You love it. Stay with it. I'm here if you need me."

"Thanks, chief."

I stuffed the phone back into my pocket and considered my options. What did I need to know first?

What had happened to the belt that was in the display case.

How could I find out?

By wheedling it out of someone in security.

But who?

I thought back through my day, remembering the guard I'd seen interviewing Bonnie and Savannah right after the lockdown was announced. Calvin. His name was Calvin, according to Dale. I bet he knew what was going on. I didn't have to tell him I was a reporter, either, because getting the information was more important than having an attributable quote.

I wandered through the house, checking the corners, but not finding the face I was looking for. What I did notice was that my fears about the crowd were founded. I saw three different guards gesturing helplessly and smiling while tourists chewed their asses about not being allowed to leave. I heard the phrase "this is still a free country, young man" in two of those conversations. Damn. I checked my watch. Pierce had warned me it would be a while, and I wondered if the cavalry would arrive before the mutiny began.

As much as that worried me, it also gave me an idea. A quick Google search on my phone told me Graceland's guards weren't sworn peace officers, which meant they weren't required to have training in law enforcement. They just had to pass a background check because they carried keys and handled cash. Other than that, they were mostly docents for the tourists, handling issues and providing directions. Which could be good for me. Actual cops are notoriously more tight-lipped than your average folks.

I finally found Calvin in the back corner of the kitchen. Smiling, I wandered over.

"Do you know where I might be able to get a bottle of water?" I asked.

"You're the third person who's asked me that. We usually send people over to the cafe, but it's locked. There is a water fountain near the restrooms out back."

I nodded. "Thank you. Do you know how much longer it'll be before they let us out of here? Funny, how excited I was to get here, but something about being locked in makes you want to get out."

"You and everyone else." He looked around nervously.

And there was my way in.

"It seems like the best way to keep everyone happy is to figure out what's going on," I said, casting my eyes down and looking up at him thorough my lashes. "Figuring things out is all about asking the right questions. I have a knack for that, you might say. How about the coins that have disappeared from the gift shop? Has anyone suggested that the missing belt is related to that?"

"Of course they have." He waved a hand in front of his face, too busy watching for a tourist uprising to wonder how I knew about any of that. "That's the first place everyone went to when they pulled the fake belt out of the box."

Switch scam. Check.

"But have they found the real one yet?" I asked. "I mean, that's got to be the reason we're all locked in here, right? Not to alarm y'all, but it looks like folks are getting restless."

"No one has come up with diddly," he said, eyeing an older man who stood in the doorway pulling at his collar and glaring our way. "But they say it couldn't have left the property, because it was cleaned and returned to the case early this morning."

"And it was cleaned on the property?" I wanted a notebook and pen, but didn't dare reach for them. He talked absently as he looked around the kitchen.

"Yeah, there's a room downstairs where they clean and polish things. I guess even in the cases, they get dirty after a while."

The room I'd heard the bickering coming from, maybe? Hot damn.

I glanced up at the unobtrusive black eyeball in the middle of the ceiling, having noticed several hundred like it as I walked through the house.

"Does the security footage show who took it out or put it back?" I asked.

"I haven't seen it. But I hear it just magically disappeared." His attention snapped back to me. "Why are you so interested in the particulars? And how do you know so much?"

Damn.

"I work with the police." Every word true. Just a few omitted. "Here's what I think: you're looking for someone who knows how to mess with the cameras and has access to the display cases or the cleaning room. Which means it may be one of your own."

I left him pondering that before he could ask me any more questions, pulling my pad and pen out as soon as I got out of his sight and scribbling so fast my fingers cramped.

So the crook was tech savvy, because the security footage had been altered. And the belt was indeed stolen, but probably still on the property thanks to little Savannah and her enthusiasm. Also, the fake was shoddy if the jarring from a little girl's right hook was enough to break it. Which meant this was not a master criminal. Which seemed contradictory.

I really wished I could talk to Chief Dale, but considering Calvin's comment about the altered security footage, no way I was going there. Which left me with two options: sit back and wait for the cops to arrive, or go look for the cleaning room.

I wasn't sure how much trouble I could get in for trespassing in a staff area, particularly one that was involved in a crime, but something told me it was a fair amount. I could get around being in the hallway earlier with an "I got lost," but that would be hard to sell a second time. On the other hand, this was a helluva story, and I had the kind of exclusive access that doesn't come along very often.

I ducked into the ladies' room to splash cold water on my face. The violet eyes that looked back at me from the mirror were ambitious as ever, but I didn't feel like spending my holiday in jail.

"What does it really get me?" I asked. "Even if I crack the story and land the scoop, is anyone but Bob going to care?"

Since it was Christmas week, there was a good chance Bob and my mom were the only two people who would even notice.

My cell phone buzzed as I walked out of the bathroom.

"Just got off with the AP," Bob's text read. "They're streaming and live tweeting your updates for the rest of the day. You just went national, kiddo. But no pressure."

My jaw dropped as I stared at the screen, reading the message a dozen times. Sweet cartwheeling Jesus. I rolled my eyes Heavenward. "Point taken," I muttered, turning for the stairs to the basement.

Christmas week meant slow news. Even so, a story blasting live over the wires comes along maybe a handful of times in a career.

National feed is the kind of chance you do not blow.

6
––––––––

Suddenly painfully aware of the cameras dotting the ceiling, I made my way back to the "staff only" door in the basement. One of several reasons I'd make a lousy criminal: I'm too nervous about getting caught, which is the kind of thing that usually gets people caught.

I reached behind my head and unfastened the clip in my hair, letting the thick waves fall around my face. I wasn't sure how much good that did, but it made me feel disguised, anyway. Leaning on the door, I tried to remember if I'd seen the little camera eyes in the staff hallway before, but couldn't.

National feed. I closed my eyes and took a deep breath, pushing on the door handle and slipping through.

Dear Santa,

All I want for Christmas is to stay out of jail.

Love, Nichelle.

I held the door so it whispered closed behind me, scanning the acoustic ceiling tiles for surveillance. I didn't see any. But just because the hallway wasn't monitored didn't mean the rooms weren't. I strode to the second door, where I'd heard the bickering, and eased it open. No camera that I could see. I slipped inside, thanking Santa silently for early Christmas gifts.

This wasn't a cleaning room. It looked like an employee locker room. Damn. All that told me was that the women I'd overheard worked here, which I had already assumed. I looked around at the shiny banks of lockers, wondering if the missing belt was hidden in one. That seemed an obvious place to hide it, but would security think to look there? Since I had no way to get past a hundred padlocks, I would have to hope they did. I started to turn back for the hallway before I spied a trash can in the corner. Evidence often turns up in the trash, and security had been awfully busy running interference with tourists. Maybe they hadn't gotten around to examining the garbage. Since this wasn't a public area, chances were at least even that the trash was only emptied every few days.

I put an ear to the door, not hearing anyone in the hallway.

Striding to the trash can, I pulled the lid off and set it on the floor behind me. The can was about three-quarters full of a jumble of coffee cups and empty soda cans.

I pushed my sweater sleeve up and reached inside, sifting through the refuse and reminding myself that the sloshing liquid was just old coffee. Which was the most interesting thing I found.

I washed my hands in the corner sink and slumped on a bench. Where else could I look? I ticked through the pieces of my puzzle again, letting my head fall back and sighing. The ceiling was acoustic tile, the speckled kind that lifts in and out of a grid. My eyes wandered to an abnormality in the one on my right. It had a blank chunk in one corner, with no speckles. But the longer I stared, the more it looked like something covering the tile. I threw a glance at the door and climbed up on the bench, stretching on tiptoe and thanking God for my height and my heels as I pushed the square up and pulled a piece of folded paper from behind it.

Hopping down, I unfolded it.

It was a diagram of some sort, printed front and back on a piece of computer paper. Studying it for a minute, I figured out it was a schematic for plumbing and ductwork.

I eyed the large vent overhead. Could the belt be hidden in the heating ducts? There were probably miles of them in the house, which certainly made it smart for someone who knew the layout. But I couldn't just go crawling through the ductwork because one: that's a lot more dangerous than it looks on TV, and two: Dale the security chief, who might be the crook, knew I was a reporter.

I folded the diagram carefully and slid it into a side pocket on my bag. It was worth hanging onto until the cops showed up, just in case.

I peeked back out into the hallway and dropped the door closed again when I saw two women in housekeeping uniforms headed for the main house. I waited until I heard the heavy door at the end of the hall close and tried again. All clear.

Since I hadn't seen a camera (or another person) yet, I figured my "I got lost" defense might still fly, and the paper hidden in the ceiling had given me an idea. I turned back to the main part of the house to check out vent covers. I wasn't playing Bruce Willis comes to Graceland, but maybe I could tip off Detective Pierce if any of them looked like they'd been tampered with.

My cell phone buzzed just as I reached for the door handle at the trophy hall (always start at the scene of the crime), and I snatched it up, hoping Detective Pierce was calling to say the cavalry was headed my way.

Not the same number I'd called, but a Memphis area code.

"Clarke," I said, pressing it to my ear.

"Miss Clarke, this is Man-Margaret, out here at the Heartache Motel?"

Okay. "Hey, Margaret. What can I do for you?"

"Well, I've had a couple of calls this morning about your dog," she said. "Are you still in the hotel?"

"I am not," I said, Darcy's uncharacteristic yipping from the night before flashing through my thoughts. "Crap, is she barking again?"

"She's being a little mouthy this morning, which is certainly her right as a female, but it's disturbing some of the other guests."

"Damn. I'm so, so sorry. I'm locked in at Graceland. There's been a theft here and they're not letting anyone in or out right now."

"A theft? From the King's home?" The speaker on my phone practically dripped curiosity and horror, they coated her words so thickly.

"A belt he wore on stage. From the trophy room."

"My stars."

I switched back to Darcy. I didn't want her up there annoying people, and I had less than no way to address that.

"Margaret, I don't suppose you would consider going into my room and checking on Darcy for me?" I asked. "She almost never barks. The furnace rattling seemed to be bugging her last night, and that might be it."

"Sure thing. I'll call you back if anything's wrong, sugar. Get a picture of the Christmas tree for me."

"I'll do it. Thank you."

I stuck the phone back into my pocket, wondering what

the hell was wrong with my dog before I turned my attention back to the more pressing question at hand. I pulled open the door to the trophy room, hoping Margaret would take good care of my little furry princess.

The trophy hall was still packed, the wall of guards standing sentry at the empty case.

I scanned the ceiling for air vents and found them spaced about every six feet along the top of the perimeter wall. I walked along, studying awards and gold records and sneaking peeks at each vent cover, trying not to be too obvious. The first four obviously hadn't been touched in years, with even a bit of rust on the screws that held them in place.

The fifth one had no rust. And new paint over the screws. I stepped closer, standing on tiptoe and peering up into the vent.

A tiny red light winked. I tottered closer—walking on pointe in stilettos verges on circus-worthy.

A tiny red light with a tiny lens next to it. Holy shit. It was a bitty video camera that no one who wasn't looking for it would ever notice. I'd seen my colleagues in TV journalism use them for investigative stories.

Santa Claus is coming to town, indeed. Pieces of my puzzle rained into place.

I spun around, already sure the camera in the vent was trained on the case the belt had been in. That's how the video feed was spliced. Check.

I reached for the schematic I'd found and then thought better of it, turning to go back outside and away from the crooks' camera before I checked it. My fingers itched to call Detective Pierce back.

Teresa was talking to one of the guards in front of the display case, and she smiled and waved.

"Hey there, Richmond," she said, crossing the floor to

meet me. "How are you liking Graceland? I'll say this: it's usually not this exciting around here."

"I was going for the regular tourist experience," I said, stepping sideways out of the camera's line of sight. "But this is good, too."

She looked around. "It's been ninety minutes already. I wonder how much longer it will be before people get mad about being kept in here?"

"About when they start to get hungry, I imagine," I said. "I hear the police are on their way."

"Well, I can tell you that a big gold and jeweled belt goes in that case they're standing in front of. It's one of my favorite pieces. And it's not there. But how in God's name they think anyone could have gotten it out without breaking the case is beyond me. Can you believe one of these people could be a thief?" She gestured to the crowd.

Wait. I hadn't considered the possibility that the culprit was a tourist, because what I knew pointed to someone on the staff. But what if this was all going down today because of someone else who was here? Maybe someone who was supposed to help the staff member smuggle the belt off the property while the fake sat in the case?

"How would a tourist get the thing out of there, though?" I wondered aloud.

Teresa considered that. "I don't know," she said finally. "I guess that's why I'm not a thief. Can you imagine how much a person would have to love Elvis to want something like that?"

"A person would just have to love money," I said. "Imagine how much that belt would be worth to the right collector." I scrunched my nose with distaste. Even if the house was a museum, it felt akin to grave robbing, which oozes squicky criminal factor.

I thought about her Elvis wall, wondering.

"Hey Teresa, you don't happen to have a photo of that belt back home, do you?" I asked. Without knowing which one I was looking for, I hadn't bothered to search online. If she had a neighbor who could send her a copy of a photo, art to go with the story confirming the theft would be a big plus for wire feed.

"Only about twenty," she said. "I even took one with my new camera this morning."

My breath stopped. "You what?"

She opened her fanny pack and fished out a small silver Nikon digital. It beeped when she powered it up, and she flicked through pictures for a few seconds, then handed it to me.

I tossed Santa another quick mental *thank you*, trying to figure out how I could get the image to my photo editor back in Richmond. "I don't suppose there's any way for us to get an older picture to put next to this one, is there?"

"All mine are in a shoebox on my Elvis wall in Florida," she said. "But there are a dozen books in the gift shop about the mansion. Surely there's one in there."

I resisted the urge to kiss her brightly-rouged cheek. "You, Teresa, are a genius."

Why hadn't I thought to check out the gift shop earlier? The coin scam was going on there, right? I wanted a look at the coins. Hopefully, I'd find a picture of the missing belt to go with this one my new friend had unknowingly snapped of the fake. And maybe I could find a lead on catching the thief while I was at it.

7

I crossed another walkway to the little building where Graceland Gifts was located, smiling at the Christmas homage to Elvis in the front window (which included a giant cardboard cutout of him in a Santa suit driving the black Cadillac from *It's Christmastime, Pretty Baby*) as I walked into the shop.

"Welcome to Graceland," the clerk behind the counter said. "You looking for anything special today?"

Yes. But I didn't want to talk to him about that just yet.

"Just browsing," He returned his attention to an open magazine on the counter. I eyeballed him. A little over six feet with a slight build and slicked-back hair, this guy probably hadn't been alive at the same time as Elvis, but his hair and lip curl said he idolized the King. Could he be the thief? Eh. Maybe. He worked here in the gift shop, where the thefts had started. But that wasn't a reason to break out the handcuffs.

I spied a bookshelf in the corner and hurried to it through the crowd of bored tourists, pulling out a book about the house. I flipped through it, but couldn't find a picture of anything that looked like the belt I'd seen in Teresa's photo. My interest was in how careful the fake was. Not that I really knew what I'd do with that information, but it could be handy to have.

I went through three more books before I found one with a chapter on costumes, and I flipped eagerly to the first page. Right square in the middle of it, under the chapter heading, was a large leather belt glittering with gold and jewels. The text told me Elvis hadn't worn real diamonds around his torso. But the gold, the book said, was real. Was the same true about those coins?

I pulled out my phone and opened my eBay app. I was pretty practiced at finding stuff there, because it was where most of my designer shoe collection had come from. I searched for "Elvis coin" and came up with several hundred hits. Pierce said the stolen ones didn't have a fencing report, though. So either the cops hadn't found them, which seemed unlikely if I could do it with a simple search, or these silver Franklin Mint ones weren't what they were looking for.

My shoe money was on the latter.

I found the display in a locked glass case on the back wall. And I was right: they weren't just any limited-edition coins featuring Elvis' face.

They were gold coins.

I opened my web browser and looked up the price of gold.

Better than twelve hundred dollars an ounce and climbing.

That was more than "Christmas money," unless Santa was feeling very generous this year. Or unless the bickering mystery women were splitting it several ways.

"Would you like to see something from inside the case?" The clerk's voice came from behind me, and nearly made me jump out of my skin.

"What kind of gold are these coins made of?" I smiled.

"And where did they come from? I'm looking for a Christmas gift for my mom."

"Depends. Some of them are pure 24-karat, some are plated," he said. "We don't mint them, if that's what you're asking. They're imported. People overseas went nutters when he died, made all kinds of limited-edition valuable things."

"Can I see a few of them?" I asked, swallowing hard. I had a feeling I'd just found the common thread in the thefts—gold —which meant they were very likely the work of the same person or people.

He pulled three out and laid them on top of the case.

I picked up the first one, inspecting the gleaming finish under the plastic casing. The face of it was imprinted with Elvis' head, the back with music notes and *The King of Rock n' Roll.* I weighed it in my hand. It was heavy.

"Is this one solid gold?" I asked.

"Good eye." He grinned. "It is."

"Do you have certificates or something for them?"

"Of course." He picked up a portable file and opened it, laying a thick, orange and gold rimmed paper on the counter. It claimed the coin I was holding was number sixty-four of two hundred fifty made in Australia in 1993.

"Are these the only collectible coins in you sell here?"

"Yep."

"And they're always locked in this case?"

"Yes, ma'am." His eyebrow went up a little.

So whoever was switching them had a key. Or was handy with a lock picking kit.

I stared at the coin, wondering if it was the real thing. And how the thieves were making the fake ones the detective had described. The answer was in finding out who took that belt, I was sure.

"How much?" I asked, sticking a hand into my bag.

"Depends on what you want," he said. "The solid gold ones are fifteen hundred, and the plated ones are between three-fifty and five hundred."

"I'm going to have to think about it," I said, handing the coin back. "But thanks for your help."

He laid them carefully back in the glass case and locked it.

"Just come back by if you change your mind," he said.

I smiled and strode out of the shop. My visit had given me an idea why the coins had just disappeared instead of being fenced. I pulled out my phone and dialed Detective Pierce.

8

"Y'all can't find where the coins are going because they're not," I said in rush when Pierce picked up. "Rather, they're not coins anymore. They're melting them and selling the gold. I think."

"Slow down," he said, background noise fading. "I missed about half of that. Who is this?"

Oops.

"Sorry. It's Nichelle Clarke from the *Richmond Telegraph*. The reporter locked in Graceland? You said earlier there was no report showing the coins from the gift shop had been fenced, right?"

"Not that I could see," he said. "It's weird, for a theft case that old."

"I think I know why," I said. "The coins aren't just any coins. They're gold, commemorative heirlooms from overseas Graceland acquires and sells in the gift shop."

"Okay." He drew the word out. "Help me catch up, here, Miss Clarke."

"I was just over there looking at them, and looking at photos of the belt that's gone," I said. "The thing they have in common is that they're gold. Gold is ridiculously high right now."

"They're melting it!" He might as well have shouted "Eureka!" and he was so loud I almost dropped the phone.

"Bingo. It wouldn't be worth quite as much as these things retail for, but it's close enough because gold is so high right now. And a great way to skirt getting caught, especially if they're swapping them out with fakes, like you said."

"No wonder my buddy said you were trustworthy," Pierce said. "You're quite a detective yourself."

"There's more. I found a schematic of the air ducts and went back to the trophy room to look at the vents, and there's a camera in one of them, trained on the empty display case. Semi-pro, too, because it's the kind of camera I've seen TV folks use on investigative stories. They're not cheap. Anyway, one of the guards told me earlier that the security feed was spliced. That's how. Maybe y'all can get prints off of it?"

"I am thoroughly impressed, Miss Clarke." I heard computer keys clicking.

"Just chasing the story," I said. "But thanks."

"I saw your report come up on CNN a little while ago," he said. "I did request a unit out there. It shouldn't be long now. I hope."

"I think I'll keep leaving that out," I said. "The natives are getting restless here. I've seen several people chewing out various security folks."

"I see," he said. "Well, you've certainly been a help to me, so what can I do for you?"

"Can I get a comment on the record about the gold investigation?"

He cleared his throat. "I can confirm that the Memphis Police Department is looking into the possibility of a theft ring operating out of Graceland," he intoned.

"Thank you, detective."

"Thank you, Miss Clarke. Let me get back to the station and I'll see what I can dig up. They have to have someone processing the gold for them. I'll call you if I come up with who or how."

I hung up and dialed Bob.

"I need to get some photos to Larry," I said when my editor picked up. "Has he gone on vacation yet?"

"I don't know," Bob said. "You have art?"

"I do. Page him quick, then I'll fill you in."

He clicked me onto hold.

"He's waiting," he said when he came back on the line.

"The first one is easy. I took it with my phone," I said. "But I need him to check something out, and the other one is on a camera that belongs to a lady I met, and I need Larry to have it at full resolution. Any ideas?"

Bob blew out a short sigh. "I don't suppose you have your laptop?" he asked.

"Not on me."

"Let me ask Larry. Send him what you've got and what to look for."

I clicked off the call and called up the photo I'd taken of the image in the book, attaching it to an email in the highest resolution my phone would allow. The "sending" bar inched across the screen, and my phone beeped the "low battery" signal.

Shit. I clicked the screen dark.

I wasn't sure what I wanted Larry to look for, to tell the truth. I wanted to know how good a fake the belt in Teresa's photo was.

I thought about Dale and the mysterious women I'd overheard, wondering again if they might be in cahoots, stealing coins, or the belt—or both.

Then there was friendly Elvis the gift shop clerk, who knew an awful lot about the coins.

And, you know, about a hundred other people I hadn't had a chance to talk to or gauge suspicion of. And that was just employees. Though I was pretty sure the culprit worked at the mansion.

"You don't seem to understand," a pleading voice broke my concentration. "I have to go out to my truck."

I whirled, looking for the source of the commotion, and found an older man in jeans and a golf shirt squaring off with the guard I'd talked to in the kitchen earlier.

"My wife needs her heart medication. It's an emergency. We didn't bring it in because we thought we'd be back over there for lunch."

Damn. Mutiny, ahoy. Which would make a great story, when I wasn't stuck in the middle of it.

"Sir, we're so sorry for the inconvenience," Calvin said, trying to keep a soothing tone. "If you'd please just stay with us a little longer. We're happy to offer you a pass to return another day, too."

Way to miss the point, Calvin.

"Won't do me no good to have a pass if my wife has a heart attack because of your nonsense." The man cast a worried glance at a woman on a bench along the outside west wall of the house. She was leaning back, eyes closed.

Double damn. I didn't want anyone to end up in the hospital, and I knew no one else here did, either. The guard was a nice guy. Maybe he just didn't understand.

I caught the guard's gaze over the man's head.

His eyes betrayed confused helplessness. I could tell he wanted to do something, but he wasn't sure about getting in trouble with his boss.

I was interested to see how Dale would handle this situation, too. I strolled over and offered a smile. "Is there a problem, gentlemen?"

"There's gonna be if he don't get me the hell out to my truck," the man said.

"Why don't you call someone and see what you can do about that?" I smiled at the guard. "I know no one wants to see this situation become any more difficult. It could turn into a PR nightmare if someone gets sick, and that isn't in anyone's best interest, right?"

The guard nodded and fumbled a handheld radio from his tool belt.

The man smiled at me. "Thank you."

"No problem," I said. "I think everyone's on edge today."

He scurried over to his wife and I retreated to a corner, stepping behind a large rubber plant. Dale was there in less than three minutes. He smiled and put a hand out for the man, then gave the woman a concerned once-over. After a quick conference with the guard, he took the man's car keys and walked toward the gate, and my heart took off at a gallop.

What if it was him and he was about to get the belt off the property? I tossed a glance at the couple. Shit, what if they were in on it, too?

The man turned to tend to his wife, and Calvin hustled back inside, probably ecstatic to be rid of the whole situation. No one was watching Dale. What better cover for smuggling something out of a lockdown?

I took off, keeping my eyes on his big hat.

Hanging back, I watched as he let himself out the gate and crossed Elvis Presley Boulevard. He locked the gate behind him, and when I was pretty sure he wouldn't notice, I crept over to it and looked through. He wandered through the parking lot clicking the key fob, finally stopping next to a battered midnight-blue Silverado when its headlights winked.

He wasn't carrying anything, and the only place I could see him possibly hiding the belt was under his hat.

I couldn't see what he did behind the door, but he didn't remove the hat. He also didn't seem to be in there very long, and he did come up with a pill bottle. So much for that theory.

As he crossed back to the gates, a satellite truck rounded the corner and pulled to a stop across the street. Dale glanced at the Donna-Karan-suited reporter and jogged back across the street, waving a "no comment" as he locked the gates. He charged past me without so much as a single glance, appearing intent on both getting away from the cameras and getting the lady her medicine.

I watched the reporter turn to her cameraman, pointing to the things she wanted shots of. Another truck turned into the parking lot, this one with an NBC logo. I wasn't too worried about it yet. I'd expected other reporters to show up when the story hit the wires. I was still the only one inside.

I jogged to catch up with Dale. He took the medication to the woman and disappeared back inside the house.

I leaned my head against the wall and closed my eyes. Strike two. Well, maybe. It didn't rule Dale out, but the old couple was clean.

My phone buzzed, and I raised it to my ear.

"Bob said you need to send more photos?" Larry asked when I picked up.

"I do. And my phone is almost dead. Thanks for hanging around. I don't know how to get the pictures off this little old lady's camera to send them to you. I'm hoping you have a magic trick for that."

"Depends. What kind of camera?"

"A teeny little Nikon digital."

"You have a Blackberry, right?"

"Yes, but I can't take pictures of her pictures for you. I want the higher resolution, and I also can't kill my battery."

"But you can put her micro SD card in the slot on the side of your phone and copy them off to me. Though I can't help with the battery," Larry said.

"I can?" Is that what the bitty little slot on my phone was for?

"It should work. Most of those little cameras use the micro technology." Larry said.

"You're brilliant," I said. "Drinks are on me next time."

"Awesome. What do I look for when I get them?"

"I want to know how good the copy in her pictures is of that belt I already sent you the photo of," I said. "And then ... anything out of place."

"Gee, that's not vague," he said with a chuckle. "You got it, Lois Lane. Bob says we're feeding to the wires. I'm happy to help. Go get 'em."

"I'm giving it my all. Thanks, Larry." I hung up and charged back inside, looking for Teresa.

9

Teresa was sweet about loaning me her memory card, which was just as teeny as Larry said it would be and slid right into the port on the side of my phone. Score one for technology.

I thanked her and warned her against adding to her coin collection on this trip. She raised an eyebrow, but nodded and waved as I turned to my email.

I highlighted the thumbnails of about ten photos taken in the awards hall that morning and attached them to an email to Larry, cringing when the battery percentage dropped to seventeen. I couldn't turn the phone off, because detective Pierce might try to call. Plus, I needed to send Bob an update. I turned the screen brightness down so far I could barely see text, opened an email, and started typing.

Memphis police continued to search for suspects Friday as suspicion mounted that a theft ring was operating out of Graceland Mansion.

"I can confirm that the Memphis Police Department is looking into the possibility of a theft ring operating out of Graceland," Det. Lionel Pierce of the MPD said.

The Telegraph *has learned that the items missing from Grace-land—several collector coins, according to police, and a belt Elvis wore onstage, an unnamed Graceland security guard confirmed—have one thing in common: they're all made of gold. At noon Friday, the precious metal was trading at more than $1200 an ounce.*

Inside Graceland, tourists have been kept on the property for going on two hours, and security officers are starting to have difficulty with people wanting to leave. So far, officers have been able to keep everyone calm, but this reporter has witnessed a couple of tense moments. One man was upset because his wife needed medication that was left in the car, and he wasn't allowed to retrieve it.

Acting Head of Security Dale Leonard diffused the situation and went to get the medication himself.

I finished typing the story, elaborating on the scene inside the mansion and finishing with a promise for more updates soon. After I sent it, I clicked my phone off and pocketed it.

Dale.

The gift shop clerk.

The mysterious women in the locker room.

Someone else I hadn't noticed, maybe.

I cataloged what I knew, which was that the crooks were tech savvy (the camera, plus the spliced video footage) and smooth enough to pull this off for months before anyone even noticed. They knew good stuff from junk. They knew the buildings and had been in the locker room. They had access to the belt and the coins.

That meant they had to have a plan for getting that belt off the property. And before the police arrived—assuming they thought the police were coming.

I didn't want it to be Dale. He'd been so good with the little girl, Savannah, and charming with the sick woman's husband, too.

But security probably had access to the display cases. And the gift shop.

My phone buzzed, and I pulled it out and clicked it on hurriedly, trying to squeeze every second out of the battery.

"Clarke," I said.

"Nichelle, this is Detective Pierce from the Memphis PD," he said. "Listen, since you've been so helpful, I have something for you."

I caught my breath, scrambling for a pen and paper. "What's that, detective?"

"You said the thieves got around the security system, right?" he asked. "So, I have a lead on a computer hacker who's done time for something similar. Got out about eight months ago and went to work in this seedy little motel bar. The kind of place where you can imagine ready access to just about any kind of crook you'd want."

No way.

"I think I can picture it. What's the name of the place, detective?"

"I'd rather not alert them that we're looking into it."

"Off the record," I said hastily. "Please."

"The bar is called Suspicious Minds. It's in the lobby at the Heartache Motel out off I-40."

"Son of a bitch," I mumbled, scribbling. Not that I was likely to forget that, but ... Habit.

"What's that?" Pierce asked.

"Nothing. Sorry. Thanks so much for the heads up, detective. I'll call you back. And the sooner y'all can get a car out here, the better."

"Dispatch tells me there should be a unit en route inside fifteen minutes."

"I'll take it. Thanks," I said.

I clicked off the call and locked the phone, considering what he'd said.

Had I seen anyone from the motel here today? Not that I had noticed.

What had I seen at the Heartache?

Drag queens. Sex diagrams. Stinky carpet. A drug deal at the bar.

A drug deal at the bar! What if it wasn't a drug deal? What if the coins were being passed through there? I couldn't see how many or what kind of bills the blonde had passed that kitchen guy.

I racked my brain for anything helpful I might've seen and heard in Suspicious Minds, but kept coming back to the lilting lisp of Natalie Wood at the bar. After a few minutes of trying in vain to focus on the men the blonde had joined, I gave up and let my brain wander to Natalie. Why was her voice bugging me?

Hot damn. Because she sounded like the gardener I'd bumped into twice that morning. The lisp, the drawl—it matched.

I pictured both faces, but it was hard to transpose gender in determining if they were the same person.

I sat bolt upright on the bench, fishing for my phone and dialing the hotel's front desk.

"Heartache Motel, have a Blue Christmas," Man Margaret drawled.

"Margaret, it's Nichelle Clarke. In room five-twenty-eight, with the dog?"

"Hey there, sugar, what can I do for you? I just adore this pooch of yours. Want to guess why?"

"She's great, isn't she?" I said hastily. "Listen, can you tell me if Natalie is working in the bar today?"

"Sure is," she said. "Been here since noon."

Shit. I slumped back against the wall.

"You still stuck at Graceland?" Margaret asked.

"I am, and I'm so sorry, but I have to go. I'm running out of battery and I need my phone. Thanks so much for helping out with Darcy, really. I'm sorry she was being a pill. She's not usually like that. I'll see you soon."

I hung up, running back through my latest blown theory.

If Natalie was at the Heartache, then she wasn't here being a gardener. So much for that.

Except.

I checked my watch.

Man-Margaret said Natalie came in at noon. That was about an hour ago, and strictly speaking, I hadn't seen my coverall-suited friend since before that.

Was he still here? Or was the belt on its way to be melted because he knew a way off the property? He worked the grounds, after all. And he'd been carrying a big bucket out of that downstairs hallway where the cleaning room was right before everything went bat-shit that morning, too. What was that about?

I stood and looked around, wondering where I could even start to hunt for him. And also wondering if I was crazy.

There were reporters at the gate, and the cops were on their way. My exclusive was about to evaporate, and I wasn't sure the police would believe me about the gardener. Clock ticking, I wandered around the corner of the house and surveyed the golf-course worthy blanket of winter rye. Out on the far corner of the property, I spied a guest-house sized gardening shed, surrounded by beautiful beds full of winter-blooming flowers. The barn-style doors said it was likely Graceland landscaping HQ.

I bet it was also off the security camera grid. The perfect

place to hide stolen treasure, if you knew your way around. The guy had said he was working alone.

I started across the lawn and my phone buzzed again.

"Clarke," I answered.

"Nicey, it's Larry. Listen, I think I got something here for you."

I stopped.

"What's that?"

"Well, first off, if this thing in these photos is a copy of that one you sent me, it's a pretty damned good one. I pulled it up as far as I could, and I can only see tiny differences. Spacing in the rhinestones in some places, color of the leather that might even be the different cameras."

So the knockoff was a good ringer. Which meant this could have gone unnoticed for a while if little Savannah hadn't whacked the glass. That meant it was part of a long-term scheme, because really, if you just wanted to steal something, why would you go to the trouble to replace it? You wouldn't, unless you wanted the opportunity to do it again. I stared at the gardening shed, taking a step forward.

"Thanks, Larry. Anything else jump out at you?"

"A couple of people are in most of the photos you sent me from the camera you borrowed," he said. "Not sure what it means, but there's a security guy in a big hat who's guarding that case pretty close. Except he's not looking at it. He's looking off at other stuff. Never more than about ten steps from your belt, though. Struck me as odd."

Damn. Facts are hard to argue with, and the more of them piled up, the more it seemed like Dale was knee-deep in this.

"Got it. I know who he is. That it? Not that I'm not grateful, but my battery situation is getting critical."

"There're tons of people on the edges of all these photos, but the security guy and one other dude, with slicked-back dark hair, are the only two who show up in all of them," he said.

"What's he wearing?"

"Khakis and a blue polo. Collar flipped up."

The gift shop guy. What was he doing out there?

Hot damn, indeed.

I thanked Larry again and hung up, checking my battery. Twelve percent. Crap. I turned back for the main house, then stopped again.

Even if it was Dale and the gift shop Elvis in cahoots, I couldn't prove that. Not without more evidence.

And I couldn't shake the gardener out of my head. Maybe it was all three of them. If the belt was in the garden shack, I had something to go on. And if it wasn't ... Well, that didn't prove anything, but I was no worse off for going to look. Plus, my gut said the gardener was gone, working the bar at the Heartache as Natalie Wood. Which, on the whole, I thought sounded brilliant. I just wasn't sure if it was true.

I glanced around as I approached the landscaping shack. Not another soul in sight. I eased the door open, sunshine flooding through the cute little four-pane windows that decorated every wall. It was like a gardening dollhouse. A large tub like the one I'd seen Captain Coveralls carrying that morning would be a great place to smuggle a stolen artifact out of the house.

At first glance, I didn't see any tubs in the shed, but there was a whole wall of cabinets along the back of the room. Stacks of tools lined the other two walls. I started flipping cabinets open, but didn't see anything out of the ordinary. Tools, plant food, weed killer. Certainly nothing sparkly.

I kept going, until the last set of cabinets on the lower right wouldn't budge. I curled my fingers around the tops of the door frames and yanked on both sides.

Locked.

I stepped back, opening the next set over and surveying the inside. The bottom row was the biggest, and deep enough to house that tub. What if the belt was just sitting in there waiting for things to cool off? Could I get the cabinet open? I didn't know how to pick a lock, but I had a smolderingly sexy friend who did.

And what if I got it open and the belt wasn't in there? How would I explain away being in a staff area and breaking into a cabinet?

Hopefully, Detective Pierce would vouch for me.

Why would only this one cabinet be locked?

I didn't have a good answer for that. But I figured if I'd come this far, I might as well find out.

I sighed and pulled out my phone. Twelve percent. Could Joey talk me through picking a lock in three or four percent of my battery life?

I checked the windows and door as I dialed his number. I was alone, and maybe I could peek in and scoot out without being seen if the cabinet was full of peat moss, or roundup.

The rush of adrenaline making my hands shake stemmed from the thought of what could happen if it wasn't. With national feed to the wires, blowing open a story like this and finding the belt before it made it into the melting pot? That was so far beyond huge it was hard to quantify.

And it wasn't like I'd never bent the law in the name of the news.

My pulse fluttered when Joey's voice came on the line, and I couldn't tell if it was him or the story that was more exciting. "Merry Christmas."

"Merry Christmas yourself. Do you have a second?"

"Excuse me for a moment," Joey's voice was muffled by a hand over his phone, as was the bass that replied.

"Sorry about that," he said. "Finishing up some end of year business in New York. Now, to what do I owe the pleasure? You sprung from Graceland yet?"

"No. And I have a hunch that could make my career." I reeled off the quick version of the story. "So, I need to know how to pick a lock," I finished.

"Only you, Nichelle." His words were garbled by laughter.

"Yeah, yeah, magnet for trouble. Tell me how to get this cabinet open."

"It's not really the sort of thing I can rattle off a how-to for," he said. "Some of it is feeling out the lock and figuring out how to pop it. A bit of an art form, really. But I'll do my best. What kind of tool are you working with?"

I dug through my bag.

"I have a paperclip and an ink pen," I said.

"I love a challenge," he sighed. "If you're going to keep getting into these messes, you really need some proper implements. Are you looking at the lock?"

"It's a round silver cabinet lock. About the size of a button, with a key slit splitting the middle horizontally."

"That means the inside of it is a tab lock. You have to turn it, not just pop it loose. Which is going to be damned hard to do with a paperclip."

"Of course it is." I crouched and examined it.

Joey told me to straighten the clip and put it in the far end of the keyhole, then spent five minutes talking me through how to wriggle it around. Either I was a lousy crook, or Graceland spared no expense on locks, but I got nowhere.

"Dammit," I thumped my forehead against the cabinet and shook it, and the paperclip slid in further. "Wait. I did something. It went farther into the lock."

"Good," Joey said. "Now bend it and try to get some leverage, and see if you can make it turn. Do not break it off in the lock."

I bent the clip slowly into an L-shape and wriggled it. It moved a millimeter and I almost dropped the phone.

"It's working!"

"Good. Keep going."

Five of the longest minutes in the history of mankind later, the cabinet door swung open and I gave a little yelp.

"Find what you were looking for?" Joey chuckled.

I peered inside. The bin.

"I think I might have," I breathed. "I'll call you later. Battery issues. Thanks for your help."

"It's fun to teach you things." His voice dropped a full octave and a shiver skated up my spine.

"I'm glad. I really have to hang up."

"Be careful," he warned. I promised I would and clicked off the call, sliding the bin out and holding my breath.

Empty.

"Shit!" I clapped a hand over my mouth when that popped out too loud, shoving the bin back into the cabinet and slamming the door.

Why was that worth locking up? I didn't have time to consider it before a voice came from behind me.

"What you looking for, ma'am?"

I turned slowly to find Captain Coveralls, his smile gone, thick arms folded across his chest.

Double shit.

10

Looking closer at the gardener's face, I saw Natalie, plain as day. But thinner, maybe. Or maybe he looked thinner as a man? Besides, Margaret had told me Natalie was at work.

I opened my mouth and spread my hands, unable to produce a good reply for his question

"It turns out there's a very valuable belt missing from the trophy room," I said. "I thought this looked like a good place to hide it. Away from the security cameras, with a light winter grounds keeping staff."

He didn't return my smile, giving me a critical once-over.

"I don't see anything, though," I said. "Does anything look out of place to you?"

He leaned against the inside of the door. "You. You look out of place to me, Miss Reporter. How do I know you didn't swipe that belt? Invent yourself a big ol' story for exposure? I think maybe you better be on your way back up to the house. Police car came in the gates just a minute ago. They might want to talk with you."

Damn.

"I didn't steal anything. I haven't been here before today,

and this has been going on for months," I said, my eyes lighting on his coveralls, which pulled across his middle as he leaned back.

"Is that a fact? I'm here every day, and I didn't know that." He raised his eyebrows. "How is it that you do?"

"I read a lot. Ask a lot of questions," I said, backtracking through my day to when I'd seen him that morning. His coveralls had been baggy all around when he'd waved me through the door inside the house.

When I'd seen him outside, they were snugger around his middle. Like now.

"It's not always good to ask too many questions," he said, one hand dropping to his waist as he followed my gaze. "Sometimes it gets you into trouble."

"It seems I find more than my fair share." I raised my eyes to his.

He grinned just before he lunged for me, throwing a punch. I dodged to the left and shot one foot out in an *ap-chagi*, thanking Heaven for my body combat class. My workouts were handy for more than keeping my ass fitting in my jeans.

My foot connected where his navel should have been, the heel snapping off my Louboutin boot on impact. He staggered back into the door, then tumbled through. I fell on my ass, hard, and screamed when I felt the tip of something sharp slice into the back of my thigh.

I didn't have time to be hurt. Scrambling back to my feet, I hobbled on my broken heel, looking around for a weapon. Wet warmth spread down the back of my leg, but I ignored it. A pair of hand-held trimmers rested on a workbench, and I snatched them up with shaking hands, whirling on the door as it opened.

"This is quite a story you've landed in, isn't it?" Dale. I

wasn't sure whether to be relieved or twice as scared. My pulse went with scared. Dale pulled out a Taser and trained it on my coverall-clad friend. That was a good sign.

"He's wearing it," I said, still clutching the clippers as I limped toward the door. "Under the coveralls. My heel broke when I kicked him."

The gardener's dark head dropped onto the grass, and Dale waved one arm over his head at the uniformed Memphis PD officer walking across the lawn.

Thank you, Santa. I sagged against the wall, dropping the clippers.

"The undercover detective in our gift shop tells me you've been talking to the PD today," Dale said, glancing over his shoulder at me. "He says you helped them, so I figure I'm obliged to help you. We figured the thief would try for the big score while my boss was out of town, and he did. That belt has the most gold, by weight, of any single item on the property. Paul here has done his homework."

I hobbled back into the shed, retrieving a pen and pad from my bag. Taking notes, I smiled at Dale. "I would have asked you about this, but you wouldn't talk to me this morning. And I, uh, might have had you on my suspect list."

He laughed.

"I would have had you on mine if I didn't know it was an inside job, what with all the snooping around I've seen on my security feed. We'll call it even. Whodunnit and where it was all going were the last pieces, and you helped with that. So thank you."

I reached behind me to my bleeding thigh as the officer hauled Paul the gardener to his feet and slapped cuffs on him. Dale unzipped the coveralls and retrieved the belt.

"Graceland owes you one, Miss," Dale said, nodding at me as the cop led Paul across the lawn. "How anyone could call themselves an American and want to destroy this, I have no idea."

"Money. It makes people crazy," I said, reaching a hand toward the belt. "Can I touch it?"

He smiled. "I think you've earned that."

It was heavy. And really, really cool.

11

I gave the police a statement and all my contact information. Dale loaned me a cell phone charger, and I put together a last story for Bob before I headed back to the Heartache to get Darcy.

Memphis police shattered a theft ring Friday just in time to stop a priceless piece of music history from being sold for scrap.

"We've been working with Graceland security on this investigation for months," MPD Det. Bart Sanders said. "I'm happy to report that while a belt worn by Elvis Presley in several stage performances was the thieves' latest target, it has been returned safely to its case at Graceland unharmed."

I filled in the rest of the specifics, including the tension among the locked-in tourists throughout the day and the relief when the thief was caught and the gates opened. Bob, who was always stingy with compliments, replied with a heartfelt "atta-girl" that was up there with the best Christmas gifts ever.

Turned out, the Elvis wannabe in the gift shop was undercover Memphis Detective Bart Sanders, which was why the reports in the police computer were locked. And Dale was very interested in the conversation I'd overheard that morning, because there had also been a rash of thefts from the employee locker room.

"Small potatoes, compared to this," he waved a hand in the general direction of the trophy room as he walked me to my car, "but I'd sure like to wrap that up before New Year's."

"They didn't use names, and I didn't see them," I said apologetically. "But they were both women. And they said it was 'Christmas money and Christmas is over.'"

"Thanks." He smiled.

"Thank you. This was a hell of an exclusive."

I opened the car door and paused.

"Paul doesn't happen to have a brother who works at the Heartache Motel?" I asked.

"Yep. Twin brother. Drag queen who works in the bar there. The PD has a unit headed over there to bust most of their kitchen staff, from what Bart told me. He said the detective you talked to found a whole slew of convicts there. When Paul got out of prison last year and moved here, he hooked up with them because his brother works there, and presto: theft ring."

"Was Natalie—uh, Paul's brother—in on it?"

"No criminal record, so no way to know yet," Dale said.

I smiled. "She was nice."

"Maybe she was just ignoring it because she didn't want Paul to go back to prison. It happens."

I thanked him again and eased into the car. I'd gashed my leg on gas-powered hedge trimmers, and Dale had called a female security guard up to apply antibiotic cream and a dressing. It didn't seem to be bleeding anymore, but I didn't want to irritate it.

"Come back anytime." Dale smiled as he closed the door.

"But just for the regular tour," I grinned, waving as I backed out.

* * *

I dropped my bags next to the desk and scooped Darcy up, fishing my wallet out of my bag. Man-Margaret laughed and shook her head, shooing away my MasterCard with a wave of her scarlet-tipped fingers.

"On the house, sugar. What a day. The cops hauled off half my kitchen staff, and your pooch ... she's my hero. Guess why she was raising hell at that vent? Just guess."

"Rattly furnace?" I asked, already sure from the look on her face that wasn't it.

"I sent maintenance up there to take the cover off because it popped back at her when she clawed at it. I saw it." She shook her head and my stomach lurched.

"No."

"Oh, yes. That blasted snake was in the heating vent! Animal control took it away about an hour ago. Good riddance. And you and this sweet pup are welcome here any time you're in Memphis."

I grinned. "I appreciate that."

Having seen more of Graceland than I ever intended, I was pretty sure we wouldn't return anytime soon. I smiled a goodbye in my rearview mirror and squealed when NPR quoted my story on the air ten miles into Arkansas.

"Merry Christmas to me," I sang, wondering if the politics editor at the *Washington Post* was on holiday. He was a hard guy to impress, but it would sure be nice for him to see this.

I punched the speed dial for my mom.

"I'm on my way," I said. "We're going to need coffee, but just wait til you hear this."

"I'm mixing the cookie dough now," she said. "Drive safe."

* * *

My mom flew out the front door before I'd even put the car in park, screeching despite the wee-morning hour of my arrival.

"My baby!" She swooped me into a tight hug.

We hurried into the house, swathed in its annual dose of "Christmas threw up," not a surface visible that wasn't festooned with holly or pine or some incarnation of Santa. I smelled the cookies before I remembered.

"I forgot your present!" I clapped a hand over my mouth. "I was locked in Graceland for half the day, and I forgot to get you something. I'm sorry, mom."

She grinned and shook her head, her eyes suspiciously shiny as she watched Darcy settle into the bed she kept next to the fireplace. "You're all the present I need, baby girl. Merry Christmas. Welcome home."

I hugged her again. It was good to be home. Happy and uncomplicated.

"You got a gift, though." She straightened when I let her go and pointed to the tree before she turned for the kitchen at the ding of the oven timer.

I pulled a red-foil wrapped box from beneath the branches, checking the tag. "Miss Clarke," it read.

My pulse fluttered. Or more complicated. It was too big to be a lock picking kit, though I wouldn't have put it past him if he'd had a way to get it there in the ten hours since I got off the phone with him.

"FedEx brought it, signature required and insured, with a

return address in New York." Mom scooped cookies onto a cooling rack, and I burned my mouth when I bit into one. She stared at me with raised eyebrows. "Who's in New York?"

"A friend," I said around a searing mouthful of cookie. I poured a glass of milk and perched on a barstool, setting the box on the counter.

"Aren't you going to open it?" she asked.

"I'm pretty sure you know what's in there as well as I do," I said. There was no mistaking the size or weight.

"I want to see them." She reached for the box and I swatted her hand away, pulling the paper back carefully. My breath caught just a little when I saw the spiky Louboutin logo, all the same.

"A friend, huh?" Mom poked me and I rolled my eyes and shook my head.

"It's complicated," I said.

"Because of Kyle?" she asked.

"Sort of." No way I was telling her any more. "I'm supposed to go over there tomorrow, don't forget."

I flipped the lid open and a tiny scream escaped before I could stop it, Kyle forgotten for the moment.

"Is that newsprint?" My mom breathed as I lifted the most perfect, beautiful shoes I'd ever seen from a careful bed of tissue.

"These were a limited edition," I said. "I've never seen one single pair on eBay." I slipped my right foot into a shoe, the delicious feel of never-worn artwork on my feet making my stomach flip. "Perfect."

She pulled a heavy linen card from the box.

"I tried to find something as beautiful as you," she read. "This was the closest I could get."

I snatched the card, trying to keep my breath even as I studied every line of the heavy, slanting black script.

"Who is J?" Mom's voice sounded far away. "Spill it."

"I wish I knew how to answer that." I popped the rest of the cookie into my mouth and stared at the shoes.

Crooks and murderers are far less complicated than men.

SMALL TOWN SPIN: Nichelle Clarke #3

Crime reporter Nichelle Clarke ventures out to a tiny Chesapeake Bay island community, helping a friend search for answers in the wake of unthinkable tragedy. But in small towns like this, some rocks are never meant to be overturned...

T.J. had the world in the palm of his hand. He was handsome. Popular in school. Smart. A stellar athlete. The son of super-star pro quarterback Tony Okerson, he seemed destined to follow in his father's footsteps to a career of gridiron glory.

That bright, shining dream ends when T.J.'s lifeless body is found on a rocky shoreline near his family's Chesapeake Bay home.

Due to his father's past fame, the tragedy ignites a media frenzy in the normally serene island community. Through a mutual friend, the grieving parents turn to reporter Nichelle Clarke for help. Nichelle agrees to write the story herself and attempt to quell the national media circus.

But as Nichelle begins to explore the facts surrounding the death, she discovers some shocking details. Something doesn't fit. And while the local sheriff wants to stamp the case a drug overdose and move on, Nichelle becomes convinced that foul play may have been involved.

To the townsfolk, Nichelle is an outsider, putting her nose where it doesn't belong. But in her experience, that's exactly where the most damning secrets are kept. And the further she follows the evidence trail, the more Nichelle realizes that this sleepy coastal village is anything but innocent...

ABOUT THE AUTHOR

LynDee Walker is the national bestselling author of two crime fiction series featuring strong heroines and "twisty, absorbing" mysteries. Her first Nichelle Clarke crime thriller, FRONT PAGE FATALITY, was nominated for the Agatha Award for best first novel and is an Amazon Charts Bestseller. In 2018, she introduced readers to Texas Ranger Faith McClellan in FEAR NO TRUTH. Reviews have praised her work as "well-crafted, compelling, and fast-paced," and "an edge-of-your-seat ride" with "a spider web of twists and turns that will keep you reading until the end."

Before she started writing fiction, LynDee was an award-winning journalist who covered everything from ribbon cuttings to high level police corruption, and worked closely with the various law enforcement agencies that she reported on. Her work has appeared in newspapers and magazines across the U.S.

Aside from books, LynDee loves her family, her readers, travel, and coffee. She lives in Richmond, Virginia, where she is working on her next novel when she's not juggling laundry and children's sports schedules.

Sign up for LynDee Walker's reader list at severnriverbooks.com/authors/lyndee-walker
lyndee@severnriverbooks.com

Printed in the United States
by Baker & Taylor Publisher Services